Hanukkah

Dennis Brindell Fradin

—*Best Holiday Books*—

ENSLOW PUBLISHERS, INC.
Bloy St. & Ramsey Ave.   P.O. Box 38
Box 777   Aldershot
Hillside, N.J. 07205   Hants GU12 6BP
U.S.A.   U.K.

> *For my dear friends Rolene, Alvin, Sonya, and Juliane Ferdinand*

Copyright © 1990 by Enslow Publishers, Inc.

All rights reserved.

No part of this book may be reproduced by any means without the written permission of the publisher.

Library of Congress Cataloging-in-Publication Data
Fradin, Dennis B.
    Hanukkah / by Dennis Brindell Fradin.
       p. cm. — (Best holiday books)
    Summary: Describes the history behind Hanukkah and the various ways it is celebrated.
    ISBN 0-89490-259-8
    1. Hanukkah—Juvenile literature. [1. Hanukkah.] I. Title.
II. Series: Fradin, Dennis B. Best holiday books.
BM695.H3F67 1990
296.4'35—dc20   89-25643
                                                            CIP
                                                             AC

Printed in the United States of America

10 9 8 7 6 5 4 3 2

Illustration Credits:
Tom Dunnington: p. 20; Antiochus IV coin photography by Marti Dziuban at Harlan J. Berk, Ltd., Chicago, Illinois: p. 16; Judith Bloom Fradin: pp. 33, 36, 40, 44; From the collection of the Hebrew Union College Skirball Museum, Los Angeles, Erich Hockley photographer: p. 17; Historical Pictures Service, Chicago: pp. 10, 14, 22; Jewish Museum/Art Resource, N.Y.: p. 41; Library of Congress: p. 29; Norma Morrison: p. 4; Religious News Service: pp. 8, 11, 26; Religious News Service/Richard Nowitz: p. 30; Courtesy of Spertus Museum of Judaica, Chicago, Illinois: pp. 21, 25, 32.

Cover Illustration by Charlott Nathan

Contents

Happy Hanukkah!	5
Who Are the Jewish People?	7
Antiochus IV Tries to Destroy Judaism	13
The Maccabees Strike Back!	19
The First Hanukkah	24
The Growth of Hanukkah	28
The Hanukkah Menorah	31
Hanukkah *Gelt* and Other Gifts	35
A Hanukkah Party	38
Hanukkah Will Keep Changing	43
Glossary	45
Index	47

This girl is lighting her family's menorah.

Happy Hanukkah!

Hanukkah is an eight-day Jewish holiday that usually falls in December. Hanukkah honors a victory that the Jewish people won over their enemies more than 2,100 years ago. Jews are proud of this victory. As a result, Hanukkah is a very happy holiday.

Hanukkah means "dedication," in the sense of setting something aside for God. After their victory, the Jews repaired the Temple in Jerusalem that their enemies had wrecked. They rededicated the Temple to God.

Hanukkah is also called the Festival of Lights. To honor their people's triumph of more than 2,100 years ago, Jews burn candles in a holder called a menorah during Hanukkah. Many Jewish families also hold Hanukkah parties. Gifts may be exchanged at these parties. There may be special foods, games, and songs. And someone may tell the children what Hanukkah means to the Jewish people.

Who Are the Jewish People?

To understand Hanukkah, it helps to know a little about the Jewish people (often called the Jews). They are followers of the religion called Judaism. Although Jews have their own small nation (Israel), they also live in many other countries. And although most Jews are white, there are some black Jews too.

Like all religions, Judaism has some special customs. Jews call their houses of worship temples or synagogues. Their religious leaders are rabbis. Certain foods such as pork (pig meat) are forbidden to the Jews. They have their own language, Hebrew. A part of the Bible, the Old Testament, relates especially to the Jews.

Judaism is one of the world's oldest religions. The birth of Judaism about 4,000 years ago marked a big change in religion. Earlier people had worshiped many gods. Judaism was the first religion to teach that there is one God. Everyone who believes in one God today

This Jewish boy is studying his lessons at a religious school.

can thank the Jews for starting this practice.

The Jews also gave the world the Ten Commandments. According to the Old Testament, God gave these ten basic rules for life to Moses on Mount Sinai. Two of the commandments are "Thou shalt not kill" and "Honor thy father and thy mother." The Ten Commandments have become rules for many other people besides the Jews. For example, Christianity adopted the Ten Commandments and other Jewish beliefs. This happened because Christianity grew out of Judaism. Jesus Christ, the founder of Christianity, was born a Jew.

Judaism also teaches that people should obey God and be kind to others. Several Old Testament stories tell of good people who beat a stronger enemy with God's help. One such story tells of a youth named David who fought the giant Goliath. Goliath laughed when he saw David standing with his slingshot and stones. But God knew the goodness in David's heart and helped him kill Goliath.

Moses with the Ten Commandments

David was much smaller than Goliath, but God helped him kill the giant.

Like David, the Jews have faced many strong enemies. More than 3,000 years ago, the Egyptians enslaved the Jews. Moses led the Jews out of slavery. The spring holiday Passover celebrates the Jews' escape from Egyptian slavery.

During World War II (1939–1945) the German Nazis tried to destroy the Jewish people. Although the Nazis killed six million Jewish people in Europe, the Jews as a people survived. In 1948, a Jewish nation was founded in the Jews' ancient homeland. This nation is called Israel. The United States, Israel, and Russia are the three main places where Jews live today.

Between the Egyptian and the Nazi periods, the Jews fought a king who outlawed their religion. The story of this struggle is the story of Hanukkah.

Antiochus IV Tries to Destroy Judaism

Most Americans use the Christian calendar. It counts years in relation to Christ's birth. The years before Christ's birth are called B.C. for "Before Christ." The years after Christ's birth are called A.D., for *Anno Domini* or "in the Year of the Lord."

There is also a Jewish calendar. It starts 3,760 1/4 years before Christ's birth. According to an old Jewish belief, that was when God made the world. In the Jewish calendar, the year 2000 A.D. is the year 5760. Most North American Jews use the Christian calendar in their daily lives, though. And in this book the Christian calendar is also used.

Ancient Greek people at the Temple of Zeus in Olympia, Greece

Long ago, modern Israel was called Palestine. Ancient Palestine was conquered again and again. Around 330 B.C. the Greeks seized much of Palestine. At first the Greek rulers gave the Jews a lot of freedom. They let them worship in peace and run many of their own affairs. Some Jews liked the Greek way of life so much that they gave up their Jewish customs. They dressed in Greek clothes and followed other Greek ways. Those Jews who thought this was wrong were allowed to keep their old customs.

In 175 B.C. Antiochus IV began ruling much of Palestine. He was a Greek king from Syria, which is just northeast of modern Israel. Antiochus IV did not give Jews a choice about adopting Greek ways. Starting mainly in the holy city of Jerusalem, he tried to destroy Judaism.

Antiochus IV outlawed Jewish religious services. He ordered Jews to eat pork and killed some people who refused. He wrecked religious objects in the Jerusalem Temple. He then placed statues of Greek gods inside the Temple. This act struck at the heart of Judaism. The worship of one God instead of many gods is the religion's central idea.

The king ordered Jews to pray to the Greek gods. Knowing they would die if they refused, some Jews obeyed. Others, including the legendary Hannah and her sons, chose death. It was

Although Antiochus IV died over 2,000 years ago, we know what he looked like! This ancient coin shows Antiochus IV.

The Temple in Jerusalem

said that Antiochus IV killed six of Hannah's seven sons one by one because they would not worship the Greek gods. Finally, only Hannah's three-year-old son was left. Even the cruel king wanted Hannah to be left one son. Reportedly Antiochus IV offered to adopt the boy if he would pray to the Greek gods. But the child refused, so he was killed too. It was said that Hannah then died by jumping off the Temple wall.

Some Jews rebelled against Antiochus IV. A religious leader named Jason led one uprising. The king punished the Jews for this rebellion by killing thousands of them.

Many Jews tried to escape the king by moving from Jerusalem to small villages. But Antiochus IV sent soldiers across the countryside. The troops found the Jews and ordered them to adopt Greek ways. The soldiers had a test to see which Jews were willing to give up their religion. They told the Jews to eat pork. Those who refused were killed. Finally in 167 B.C., a few soldiers came to Modin. They had no idea what was about to begin in this small village.

The Maccabees Strike Back!

Once in Modin, the king's troops put up a statue of Zeus, king of the Greek gods. They brought a pig near the statue. Then they made the men of the town gather at the statue.

Modin's religious leader was an old man named Mattathias. He, his five sons, and their followers became known as the Maccabees, which may mean "the Hammers." Kill the pig and eat it, the commander told Mattathias. Mattathias didn't move. Suddenly another man said he would kill and eat the pig. Mattathias grabbed a sword and killed this man and the commander. Mattathias's sons and other villagers then helped Mattathias kill the rest of the

Mattathias and some other men of Modin facing the Syrian soldiers

troops. This began the Maccabean rebellion.

Mattathias and his men fled Modin. They hid in the mountains. But from time to time they came down to attack the king's forces and smash the statues of the Greek gods that had been set up in the villages. They told the Jewish people to return to their own customs. Meanwhile, more and more people joined the Maccabees.

The Maccabees hid in hilly areas such as this one in modern-day Israel but came down at times to fight.

Mattathias did not live to see his people triumph. He died during the first year of the rebellion. Before he died, he placed his son, Judah Maccabee, in charge of the Jewish forces.

The odds seemed to favor Antiochus IV and his Syrian army. Most of the time the Maccabees had just several thousand men. The

Judah Maccabee leading his men into battle

Syrian army was often ten times that size! The Jews had only sticks, stones, and farm tools as weapons. The enemy had bows and arrows, spears, and armor. But Judah Maccabee was a great general. He trained his troops very well. And he made them believe that God would help them win.

Judah Maccabee led four great battles against Antiochus's troops. After the Maccabees won the first three battles, the enemy raised a mighty 25,000-man army. But the Syrians made the mistake of fighting the fourth big battle in the hills not far from Jerusalem. The Jewish army, which had grown to about 10,000 men, fought best in the hills. The Maccabees killed about 5,000 enemy troops in this last great battle of the rebellion. Like David, the Jews had beaten a Goliath!

The First Hanukkah

Judah Maccabee and his men then marched to Jerusalem. They cleaned off the blood and dirt that had been smeared on the Temple. They tore down the statues of Greek gods and repaired the Temple. Then, in an eight-day ceremony late in 165 B.C., they rededicated the Temple to God. This was the first Hanukkah.

Why did they celebrate for eight days? Each fall the Jews held an eight-day harvest festival called Sukkot. The Maccabees may have missed Sukkot a few weeks earlier because of the fighting. That first Hanukkah may have been mainly a late Sukkot celebration.

There is a better-known story about why eight

Ancient mosaic of the seven-branched menorah

Judah Maccabee and his people entered Jerusalem after beating the Syrian army.

became a special Hanukkah number. After repairing the Temple, Judah relit the menorah. The lamps in this seven-branched holder were supposed to burn constantly. It was said that Judah found enough oil to burn the lamps for just one day. By a miracle, the oil lasted eight days.

In any case, Judah and his brothers proclaimed a new yearly holiday. It would be called Hanukkah, and it would last eight days. Hanukkah would honor the victory over Antiochus IV and the rededication of the Jerusalem Temple to God.

The Growth of Hanukkah

More than 2,150 years have passed since the Maccabees began Hanukkah. The holiday has changed in that time. Many Hanukkah foods, songs, and games have become popular. Gift giving has become a common custom. But the main change has been Hanukkah's growth in importance.

For centuries, Hanukkah was a happy but small holiday. A number of other Jewish holidays were more important. Only in modern times has Hanukkah become a major holiday among many Jews. Today, Hanukkah is the yearly highlight for millions of Jewish children. And it is the best-known Jewish holiday among non-Jews.

One reason for Hanukkah's growth in America is that it comes near Christmas. It provides Jewish-Americans with the same kind of family togetherness that Christmas provides for Christian-Americans. A reason for Hanukkah's great popularity in Israel is that the

Picture from an old Jewish calendar showing a European family celebrating Hanukkah in the 1800s

Israelis feel they are like the Maccabees. They fought to create Israel in 1948. They have fought since then to protect their little nation. Hanukkah is also popular in other places where Jewish people live.

With the help of his nurse, this young hospital patient is lighting a Hanukkah menorah in modern-day Jerusalem, Israel.

The Hanukkah Menorah

The Jews had seven-branched menorahs long before Hanukkah began. The seven-branched menorah is still a Jewish symbol. A special nine-branched menorah came into use for Hanukkah. It is sometimes called a *hanukkiah*, but most people call it a Hanukkah menorah.

Today, most Hanukkah menorahs are metal and hold wax candles. The first Hanukkah menorahs used oil lamps and were probably clay. Many other materials have been used to make menorahs. During World War II the Nazis placed millions of European Jews in concentration camps before killing them. Some Jews in the camps made Hanukkah menorahs out of

The nine-branched menorah used for Hanukkah is sometimes called a *hanukkiah*, but most people call it a Hanukkah menorah.

potato halves. They used fat from their food and threads from their clothes to make candles.

There is a right way to light a Hanukkah menorah. Eight of the menorah's holders are for the candles that are lit on the eight nights of Hanukkah. The ninth holder is for the *shammash* (meaning "servant" in Hebrew). The

As the song "O Hanukkah" says, the candles "shed a sweet light to remind us of days long ago."

shammash is the candle that is used to light the other candles.

On the first night of Hanukkah the *shammash* is used to light the candle on the far right. On the second night it is used to light the first two candles on the right. Each night, another candle is added. On the eighth and last night, the *shammash* is used to light all eight candles. Special prayers are said during the candle-lighting. The candles are supposed to burn for at least half an hour.

Usually family members take turns lighting the candles. That way everyone gets to take part in Hanukkah. Most families place their menorah in a window. Passers-by can see that a Jewish family lives in the building. And they can enjoy the beauty of the burning candles.

Hanukkah Gelt and Other Gifts

The Jews didn't win total freedom right after the four big battles. It took a few more years to do this. Finally, around 145 B.C., the Jews set up their own nation. It was called Judah, and it lasted nearly 100 years until the Romans conquered it. By the time Judah was founded, Judah Maccabee was dead. His brother Simon had become the Jewish leader.

Simon Maccabee began minting coins. This made the Jews happy, for the right to mint money showed that they were free. People may have begun giving *gelt* (money) as Hanukkah gifts because of the coins that Simon Maccabee made.

Girl opening Hanukkah presents

Today, many children still receive *gelt* at Hanukkah. Tops called dreidels, candy, and books are also popular Hanukkah gifts. Many children give as well as receive Hanukkah gifts. The children may give their loved ones crafts they made at school or cards with messages of love.

Some families give gifts all eight nights of Hanukkah. In this case small gifts are usually given on seven of the nights. A bigger gift may be given on the eighth night. But most families exchange gifts on one night only, often at a Hanukkah party.

A Hanukkah Party

Many Jewish families hold a party on one of the eight nights of Hanukkah. The guests may include children, parents, grandparents, aunts, uncles, cousins, and family friends. The Hanukkah party is a chance for Jews to share the joy of Hanukkah with their loved ones.

The candle-lighting is a big part of a Hanukkah party. While the people watch the burning candles, an adult may explain the Hanukkah story to the children. Sometimes older children teach the younger ones about Hanukkah.

There are traditional foods that are served at many Hanukkah parties. Latkes (potato pancakes) are among the most popular of these.

Latkes are fried in oil. This is a reminder of the oil that lasted eight days long ago in the Temple. Most people eat applesauce and sour cream with their latkes.

Cheese is another Hanukkah food. The reason relates to a story about a cousin of the Maccabees named Judith. Like other Jewish women, Judith hid and fed the Maccabean rebels. One day she found a way to do more. She brought a food basket to Holofernes, an enemy general who liked her. The feast contained a lot of cheese and salt, which made Holofernes thirsty. Judith gave Holofernes wine to drink. After Holofernes fell asleep, Judith cut off his head! Eating cheese at Hanukkah is a reminder of how Judith helped her people.

Cookies are popular Hanukkah deserts. The cookies may be made in the shape of dreidels, candles, and other things that are linked to Hanukkah. In Israel, *sufganiyot* (jelly-filled doughnuts) are popular deserts. The Maccabees ate pastries much like these.

After everyone has eaten, there are usually Hanukkah games and songs. The best-known Hanukkah game is spinning the dreidel. A dreidel is a top with four Hebrew letters on it. The letters stand for four Hebrew words that mean "A great miracle happened there." The miracle was beating the Syrians and capturing the Temple in Jerusalem. The game is played by

As anyone who has ever eaten them knows, latkes are very, very tasty!

spinning the dreidel and seeing which letter it lands on. Each letter has a certain value. Different families have different rules for keeping score.

Most Jewish families have their own favorite Hanukkah songs. Among the most popular songs are "O Hanukkah, O Hanukkah, Come

Carved wooden dreidels made in Poland during the 1700s

Light the Menorah!" and "O, Dreidel, Dreidel, Dreidel, I Made It Out of Clay." And of course sometime during the Hanukkah party comes the long-awaited moment—the opening of gifts.

Some Jews are too poor to have a Hanukkah party or buy their children Hanukkah gifts. Just as Christians do at Christmas, many Jews help the needy during Hanukkah. They do this by giving to charity. That way needy people can have a little brightness during the Festival of Lights too.

It is also common for children to visit hospitals and nursing homes during Hanukkah. They sing and dance for the patients and visit with them.

Hanukkah Will Keep Changing

All holidays slowly change. Christmas began as a purely religious holiday. Gifts and Santa Claus had no part in Christmas. Today, gifts and Santa are very big parts of Christmas.

Hanukkah has also grown and changed a great deal. At the first Hanukkah, the menorah had seven branches, not nine. Oil lamps, not candles, provided the light. People did not give gifts during Hanukkah's early years.

Hanukkah customs will keep changing. There will be new songs, foods, and games. Yet the main idea of Hanukkah will stay the same, as it has for over 2,100 years. The Festival of Lights will always be a time when Jews celebrate their survival as a people.

Some people like to bet pennies on the dreidel game.

Glossary

A.D.—refers to the years after the birth of Jesus Christ

B.C.—refers to the years before Jesus Christ was born

century—a period of 100 years

dreidel—a top with Hebrew letters on it that is used in a Hanukkah game

gelt—money

hanukkiah—the special nine-branched Hanukkah menorah

Hebrew—the ancient Jewish language that many Jews still use

Judaism—the religion of the Jewish people; Judaism is one of the world's oldest religions

latkes—potato pancakes, a traditional Hanukkah food

Maccabee—a name first given to Mattathias's son, Judah. It was later extended to Judah's family and others who helped them defeat Antiochus IV

menorah—a candle-holder used by Jewish people

million—a thousand thousand (1,000,000)

miracle—an amazing event that is thought to show God's will

Old Testament—the part of the Bible that is especially about the Jews

pork—pig meat

rabbis—Jewish religious leaders

shammash—the candle that is used to light the other candles in the menorah

synagogues—Jewish houses of worship (also called temples)

Index

A Antiochus IV, 15, *16*, 18, 22, 27

C Christianity, 9

D David, 9, *11*, 12, 23
dreidel, 37, 40-*41*, 42

F Festival of Lights, 5, 43

G gelt, 35, 37
Goliath, 9, *11*, 12, 23

H Hannah, 16, 18
Hanukkah,
    changes in, 43
    first celebration of, 24, 27
    foods of, 38-39
    games of, 40-41
    meaning of, 5
    songs of, 41-42
hanukkiah, 31, *32*
Hebrew language, 7, 40
Holofernes, 39

I Israel, 7, 12, 29-30, 39

J Jerusalem, 15, *17*, 23, 24
Jesus Christ, 9

Judah, nation of, 35
Judaism, 7
    birth of, 8-9
    teachings of, 9

L latkes, 38-39

M Maccabean rebellion, 19, 21-23
Maccabee, Judah, 23-27, 35
Maccabee, Simon, 35
Maccabees, 19, 21-24, 28, 30, 39
Mattathias, 19, *20*, 21-22
menorah, 6, *25*, 27, 31, *32*, 33-34
Modin, 18-21

O Old Testament, 7, 9

P Palestine, 15
Passover, 12

R rabbi, 7

S shammash, 33-34
sufganiyot, 39
Sukkot, 24
synagogues, 7
Syria, 15

T Temple in Jerusalem, 5, 15, 16, *17*, 18, 24, 26, 27, 40
Ten Commandments, 9, *10*